GREAT TALES FROM LONG AGO

ROBIN HOOD

Retold by Catherine Storr
Illustrated by Chris Collingwood

Methuen Children's Books
in association with Belitha Press Ltd.

LONG, LONG AGO, GREEN FORESTS COVERED
most of the country of England. In Sherwood Forest,
near the town of Nottingham, there lived a band
of men who wore Lincoln green. They were all
wonderfully good shots with the bow and arrow,
but the best of them all was their leader, Robin Hood.
Robin had been born the Earl of Huntingdon,
but his parents had died while he was young,
and he had lost his money and his lands.
So he took to the greenwood, and became an outlaw,
killing the King's deer for food.

Note: There are many legends about
Robin Hood. I have based my story on
Joseph Ritson's *Robin Hood, A collection of
all the English Poems Songs and Ballads now
Extant* (London 1795) and other sources.

CS

W HEN ROBIN FLED FROM HIS HOME
he grieved most of all for Marian,
the lady whom he had loved since childhood.
They had planned to marry,
but when he had left for Sherwood Forest,
Marian had had to stay behind, sad and lonely.

AT LAST, SHE DECIDED THAT SHE WOULD FOLLOW ROBIN
to the forest. She dressed herself
in boy's clothes, and looked like a young page.
Then she took a sword and bow and arrows,
and set off alone to Sherwood.

ROBIN WAS ALSO WANDERING THROUGH THE FOREST.
He was disguised as a beggar.
He saw the young page practising with his bow,
and asked, "Where are you going in my forest?"
"Your forest? It is the King's forest,"
said Marian. She drew her sword,
and immediately, Robin drew his.
Then the page and the beggar fought fiercely
though Robin did not use
all his strength because his opponent was so young.

ARIAN'S SWORD CUT ROBIN'S FACE
and drew blood, and Robin wounded Marian's hand.
When he saw this, he said, "Young man,
for your age you are a good swordsman.
Come and join my band and live free
in the forest with Robin Hood."
When she heard this, Marian recognised
the man she had come to find.
"Don't you know me, Robin? I am Marian," she said.
Robin took her in his arms.
"From now on, we shall fight side by side,
and not face to face," he said.
That night the outlaws made a great feast,
to celebrate the coming of Maid Marian
to Sherwood Forest.

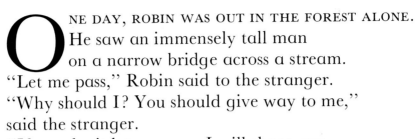

ONE DAY, ROBIN WAS OUT IN THE FOREST ALONE.
He saw an immensely tall man
on a narrow bridge across a stream.
"Let me pass," Robin said to the stranger.
"Why should I? You should give way to me,"
said the stranger.
"If you don't let me pass, I will shoot you
with my bow and arrows," said Robin.

"That would not be fair. I have no bow and arrows,
only my stout staff," said the stranger.
Robin quickly cut himself a staff
from a nearby tree. Then he and the tall stranger
began to fight on the narrow bridge.

Sometimes one seemed to be winning,
sometimes the other.
At last the stranger hit Robin so hard
that he fell into the stream
and climbed out, dripping wet.

He blew a loud note on his hunting horn.
At once his faithful band of men came leaping
through the forest, ready to avenge his defeat.
But Robin said, "No, don't attack him.
It was a fair fight. This tall man should join our band."

To the stranger, he said, "What is your name?"
The stranger said, "I am called John Little."
"You're much too tall a fellow to be called that,"
said Robin, and his men laughed and said,
"You shall be called Little John."

ONE OF ROBIN'S MEN WAS A FAT FRIAR.
This is how he and Robin first met.
Robin was riding through the forest,
when he saw a fat man sitting on the bank of a river.
Robin said to the man, "Carry me over the river,
or you shall pay well for refusing."
Without a word the fat man motioned Robin
to climb on his back and he carried him
across the river, to the further bank.
Then he said, "Now it is your turn to carry me back."
Robin agreed. He carried the fat man over the river.
The man was very heavy and Robin was out of breath
when he reached the bank. He gasped out,
"Now . . . you . . . will . . . carry . . . me . . . back again."

THE FAT MAN HOISTED ROBIN
on his back, and waded into the river.
But when he reached the middle, he said to Robin,
"Now you can swim!"
and threw him off into the water.
Robin was angry. He came back to the bank,
picked up his bow and arrows and said,
"Look out for yourself, fat man!"

But Robin's arrows could not pierce
the man's steel buckler. So they fought with swords
for a long time. At last, Robin saw
that he was going to be beaten.
He said, "Grant me a favour.
Let me blow my horn for the last time."
"You may do that," said the fat man.
Robin blew his horn and, at once,
fifty of his men came running up
and took aim at the fat man.

"Whose men are these?" the fat man asked.
"They are my men," Robin said.
"Grant me one last wish, as I granted yours,"
said the man, and he put two fingers to his lips
and whistled three times.
Immediately fifty hunting dogs came bounding
through the trees and growled at the sight
of Robin's men with their bows and arrows.

"I see that we had better be friends.
Tell me, what are you doing here
in Sherwood Forest?" said Robin.
"My name is Friar Tuck. I have come
to look for Robin Hood and to join his company,"
said the fat man.
So Friar Tuck joined Robin's band.

ONE CRISP COLD DAY IN WINTER,
Robin Hood and Little John were out in the forest,
when they saw a man wearing the dried skin
of a horse as a cloak,
which seemed to the two outlaws very strange.
"I'll go and find out what this stranger
is doing here," said Little John.
"No. I'm the leader.
I should go forward first," said Robin.
They quarrelled over this so hotly,
that Little John went off to Barnsdale,
while Robin remained in Sherwood.

LITTLE JOHN HAD JUST REACHED THE TOWN,
when he saw another of Robin Hood's men,
Will Scarlett, running out,
"I've come here just in time," he thought,
and he shot an arrow at the crowd pursuing Will.

The arrow killed the man in front, but as it went,
the bow itself broke and left Little John
without a weapon.
Will Scarlett escaped, but the Sheriff's men
took hold of Little John, and bound him to a tree.
"You shall be hanged here this very day,"
said the Sheriff.

BACK IN THE FOREST, ROBIN HOOD ASKED THE STRANGER
"What are you looking for in Sherwood Forest?"
"I have been sent by the King
to punish the outlaw Robin Hood,
for stealing the King's deer.
When I have caught him,
I shall blow on my silver bugle
and the Sheriff will know of my success," the man said.

"I will take you to where you can find him," said Robin.
"But first let us have a shooting competition."
He peeled two willow wands and
set them upright in the ground.
Then he took his place a hundred metres off and said,
"Now, come and try your skill against mine."

At his first shot, Robin missed his wand
by a hairsbreadth.
The stranger's first arrow went near, but not so near.
At the second shot, the stranger's arrow grazed
the leaf at the top of the wand,
but Robin's second arrow split his wand into two.

"You shoot wonderfully well. Tell me your name,"
the stranger said. "Tell me yours first," said Robin.
"I am Sir Guy of Gisborne, a true knight of the King's court."
"And I am Robin Hood."

WHEN HE HEARD THIS, SIR GUY DREW HIS SWORD.
Without waiting until Robin was ready,
he wounded him, and threw him down.
But Robin leapt up again and fought on,
and at last he drove his sword
through Sir Guy's body, so that the knight fell dead.

Robin changed clothes with the body and
covered it with his own green cloak.
Then he blew a single loud blast on the silver bugle.
He took Sir Guy's bow and arrows with his own,
wrapped himself in the horse-hide cloak
and set off for Barnsdale.

IN BARNSDALE, THE SHERIFF WAS READY
to see Little John hanged.
But when he heard the sound of the silver bugle,
he stopped the execution.
"That means that Sir Guy has caught Robin Hood.
When he gets here, we will have a double hanging,
master and man together," he said.
When Robin Hood reached Barnsdale,
the Sheriff thought that this was Sir Guy.

"Welcome, Sir Guy. What have you done
with that rascal, Robin Hood?" he said.
"A body with a sword thrust through it lies in the forest,
covered with Robin Hood's own cloak of Lincoln green,"
said the pretending Sir Guy. Then he said,
"As my reward, let me ask a favour.
Allow me, to hang his servant
who is bound there about to be hung."

Robin stepped up to the tree
where Little John stood.
He took out his dagger and cut his cords,
then handed him Sir Guy's bow and arrows,
and Robin and Little John together
shot at their enemies till they had all fled.
Then they returned in safety
to Sherwood Forest to celebrate their victory.